A Haunted Mess

Created by R.L. Surles

I've been told I'm a "haunt mess"

For Brandon

Created by R.L Surles

Ghostie's got it good

He's as happy as could be

He likes to keep it simple

He loves to sing and read

His hobbies keep him busy

But sometimes he feels alone

He wants to be part of the family

After all, they share this home

This family has been around for years

The days and months gone by

But no one has seemed to notice him

Not even a simple "Hi!"

He sees them reading books he loves

And hears them play his songs

It's almost like he's family

Could he possibly,

Belong?

He thinks of all the stories he's heard

Of ghosts who like to scare

Is that what he's supposed to do?

Will that make his family care?

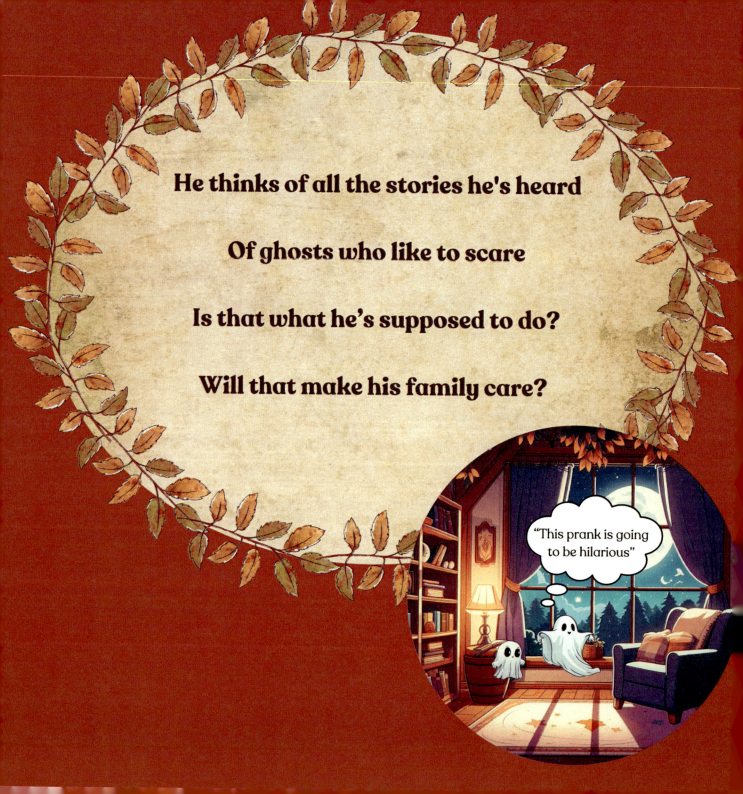

He's never liked to scare

He's tried it here and there

If he's going to do this right

He needs to prepare

He searches the shelves from bottom to top

But nothing feels quite right

He doesn't want to scare anyone

Or play cruel tricks at night

He starts to worry he's doing it wrong

A ghost who doesn't like to scare

How will his family notice him?

Will they ever know he's there?

He heads to the kitchen to clear his head

He knows he needs to calm down

He starts to feel a little better

When he sips some lemonade he found

All of a sudden he hears a scream

Someone is in distress

The family has some friends over

And they must have seen his mess

Uh Oh....

"Why is there music playing?

And why are there books on the floor?

I don't remember seeing this

When we were here before!"

Oops

The little girl just giggles

She knows who made the mess

"Don't worry it's just Ghostie

There's no need to stress"

He's always leaving messes

And playing music loud

But my parents say he's got great taste

So we don't mind that he's around

He likes to share his hobbies

He leaves things out for us to see

After all, this is his home too

So we just let him be

Ghostie couldn't be happier

That was easier than he thought

The family already knows him

And they notice him quite a lot

His life just got a little sweeter

At last, this is a real home

It's nice to feel like part of the family

And no longer feel alone

The simple act of being yourself

And sharing the things you love

Can help us all connect with each other

And that's what families are made of

Made in the USA
Las Vegas, NV
17 October 2023